FREEDA THE CHEETAH

By JTK Belle

Picklefish
Press

Printed in PRC
First Printing, 2017
ISBN: 978-0-692-94790-6

Picklefish Press
www.picklefishpress.com

JTK Belle is Jeff, Tommy, and Katie Belle.
Editor: Katie Belle
Creative Director: Tommy Belle

Book Design by
Michelle M White Graphic Design

For Mrs. Olson

1

Elephant's trunk covered both of his eyes
while the animals all ran away to go hide.

4

Across the savanna, the herd
of them thundered
as Elephant counted out
one to a hundred.

They pittered and pattered
in every direction.
They were all pretty good at
avoiding detection!

7

But the very best player of
hide-and-go-seek
was Freeda the Cheetah
of Mozambique.

She ran like the wind
and walked like the breeze

as she crouched in the grass,

and she hid behind trees.

She had stripes on her face
and brown spots all around,
and when she would hide,
she could never be found!

14

Elephant searched about
all afternoon.
He found every 'potamus,
skunk, and baboon.

17

He looked to the west, and he looked to the east.

He found every zebra and blue wildebeest.

As he crissed and he crossed
all along that savanna,

he found all the monkeys
behind the bananas.

He found every one of them, all except Freeda.

He just couldn't find that unfindable cheetah.

So all of the animals joined in the searchin',
every lion and mouse,
every turtle and urchin.

No one knows where she hides,

but they know where she doesn't,

because the places they looked

were the places she wasn't.

They looked from the lake
to the highland plateau.

"Where oh where," they cried out,
"did that crafty cat go?"

They scanned the horizon for
signs of her motion.
They looked out on the waves
of the Indian Ocean.

"Well that's it. I'm giving up now," Elephant said.
"It's time to go home and get ready for bed."

"I've had quite enough of this rigamarole,
so I'm going to get back to my watering hole."

33

But the others kept searching.
They looked all around.

They're still looking now,
but they still haven't found

the world's best player
of hide-and-go-seek—

That crafty old cheetah

from Mozambique

who runs like the wind
and walks like the breeze.

So if you happen to see her,

would you point her out please?